BLUE WILLOW

PAM CONRAD

ILLUSTRATED BY S. SAELIG GALLAGHER

PHILOMEL BOOKS • NEW YORK

For Sarah with love — P.C.
For my sweet Marty — S.G.

Many years ago, long before you were born, there was a river called Wen that flowed through the mountains, over the countryside, and past a small and peaceful village.

On one side of the Wen River, in a large mansion with rich and glorious gardens, lived a wealthy merchant. He had no friends. He hardly walked in his gardens, played no musical instrument, but he knew the number and weight of all he possessed—every grain of rice, every newborn dove, and every candle that melted away was recorded by his pointed brush on fine scrolls.

Everyone knew that he had one daughter, Kung Shi Fair, and that because his wife was dead, he treasured this daughter more than all his possessions. And it was thought by all that she was a girl who deserved such love.

Kung Shi Fair was a beautiful girl with hands as small as starfish, feet as swift as sandpipers, and hair as black as the ink on her father's scrolls. As she grew, the people of the village waited and wondered who she would marry, because they all knew that the merchant always gave her whatever she asked for.

Once she had said, "Father, I would have a moon pavilion of my very own," and he built one for her to sit in and paint her pictures. It was surrounded by peonies that filled the air with sweetness, and bamboo that sounded like wings beating in the wind.

Another day she said, "Father, I would have a boat made of cassia with fig leaf sails and a banner of orchids." And this too he had made for her, but because he loved her so much, he would not let her put it in the water.

Another time she said, "Father, I would have a stone bridge of my very own," and beneath the willow tree he built her a footbridge that led to her moon pavilion.

The favorite story of the villagers was how one day she had even said, "Father, I would like some small green frogs to waken in the morning when I cross my very own bridge," and he had sent his two servants to find small green frogs and place them beneath the bridge.

The villagers watched from the other side of the river. They were not wealthy like the merchant, neither were they poor. They were hardworking people who knew how to plow a rice field with a tired ox, and how to embroider golden dragons on silk robes with short pieces of yellow thread. They were good people who loved to see Kung Shi Fair sitting in her pavilion. Sometimes the village children would wave to her, but Kung Shi Fair would look away.

One day Kung Shi Fair was sitting in her moon pavilion when she saw something glistening on the bank of the river. She abandoned her paintbrush and carefully made her way through the bamboo and peonies to the water. When she got there, she saw it was only a broken shell. She picked it up and turned it over in her hands, then looked up and saw for the first time a boat and a young man pulling his dripping nets out of the water.

This was Chang the Good who lived across the river. He was a young fisherman who counted his wealth in nets and cormorants and the slant of the wind across the river's surface. He was a strong boy with a good heart, and the village people said of him that if in the darkness of a monsoon night you were to reach out and feel warmth beneath your hand, you would say, "Is this the shank of a hardy ox, or is this the long back of Chang the Good?" He was that strong and that steady. And that well loved.

Now Kung Shi Fair and Chang the Good were both startled to see each other. The fish spilled out of his nets, and the cormorant flapped unheeded in the air. Some say there was even the sound of bells tinkling in the slow drift of the river. The shell dropped from Kung Shi Fair's hand, and

tossing the nets on the floor of his boat, Chang the Good picked up his oars, and never taking his eyes off Kung Shi Fair, he rowed across the river to her.

When he reached the shore, Kung Shi Fair watched as he pulled the boat onto the land. She came close and touched his nets. "How beautiful," she said. "I have never seen nets this close."

"I made them myself," he told her, thinking he, as well, had never seen something so beautiful this close.

"And what a wonderful bird!" she exclaimed as the cormorant held out its wings to dry in the breeze.

"I fish with her. She dives for fish and because of the ring around her neck—and because I have trained her so well—she brings the fish to me."

"You are very clever," she said, turning her gaze full on him. The same wind that rustled her lavender silk robe tugged at his coarse, river-wet shirt. The same sand touched their feet. The same sun shone on both their heads.

"Can I tell you something?" he asked her softly.

She nodded, silent.

"One morning I came down to the river, thinking my boat would be anchored where I had left it, but it had

gotten loose in the night, and the currents had taken it away. All day long I searched along the river for my boat and could not find it. Then toward evening, when I had given up hope, I came upon a still cove, and there it was, drifting toward me. My heart swelled with love."

Kung Shi Fair tilted her head. "And so?"

"And so, this is how I felt just now, seeing you here on the bank of the river."

Kung Shi Fair frowned. "My boat has never been in the river," she said. "So I have never lost a boat, or found one." Then she smiled at him. "But I came to the river just now thinking I saw something glistening on its bank, and now I know I came for you."

Kung Shi Fair and Chang the Good were alone on the shore of the Wen River, but the people of the village have told this story ever since. This was the beginning of the story, the good, the happy part.

But it so happened that Kung Shi Fair's father was watching from the window of his mansion. His hand was tired from writing his lists, and he had risen to stretch his legs. He watched as his daughter led the fisherman across the stone foot bridge, where their footsteps woke the sleeping frogs, and he watched her lead Chang the Good to her moon pavilion.

That night he said nothing to his daughter about what he had seen. But he watched her and saw how her cheeks were high with color and how her smile came so easily. He noticed a new tenderness about her, how she touched even the flowers on the table with great care.

They were drinking their tea, sitting quietly and listening to the late summer cicadas, when one of the servants came panting onto the veranda.

"There is terrible news, Master, from down the river. It seems there is a wild leopard on a rampage. It is tearing down small houses and killing people."

"This is frightening," the merchant said. "You must tell me if you hear news of the leopard coming in this direction."

"Yes, Master," the servant answered, and he backed out of the room.

The merchant looked at his daughter. "Perhaps, until the leopard is caught, you should stay near the house and not go down into your moon pavilion."

Kung Shi Fair clapped her hands and laughed. "Don't be silly, silly father. My pavilion is perfectly safe." Then she took down her lute and played some of his favorite songs so that he would forget about the leopard . . . and about her pavilion.

The next day and every day after that, when the work of fishing was through, Kung Shi Fair and Chang the Good would meet on the shore. First they would go to the pavilion, where the silk-lined ceilings and walls rustled, and long-legged, pale green insects would watch them. Then they would trail peony petals down the path to the bridge, where they would sit and talk, and eat mulberries beneath the cool willow tree.

Finally, after many days of this, Chang the Good came with a bundle. It was a red silk bundle tied in a fisherman's knot. Without speaking, he led her over the bridge and into her pavilion.

"I have something to show you," he said. "Sit down," and she did.

Very carefully, in the late afternoon sun, he unfastened the knot and opened his bundle on the floor before her. There were jade brooches and ivory necklaces, brass bracelets, and pendants hung not on gold chains as she was used to, but on rough silk cords dull with wear.

Not knowing Kung Shi Fair had more jewelry than she could ever wear, Chang the Good held up a necklace spread in his fingers, and she bowed her head and allowed him to place it around her neck. Then another necklace and another, weighing her down. He slipped a bracelet over her small hand, and another and another. Kung Shi Fair grew quiet and still, studying his face.

He told her, "These belonged to my mother, who died when I was very young."

Now Kung Shi Fair was a rich girl, used to precious jewels and lustrous gold, and she did not know what to say about the humble pile of trinkets that Chang the Good offered her. But she could see that to Chang the Good these were great treasures, all the riches he owned. So now, with the heart of someone who has learned to love, she knew that these were the most precious gifts she had ever received.

"And this was her own ring," Chang the Good was saying, and he slipped a small jade ring onto her thumb.

"Beautiful," Kung Shi Fair told him, and she truly meant it. "I have never seen anything more beautiful."

"I want you to have them," he told her. "I want you to be my wife."

Kung Shi Fair held very still. The silk on the walls and the ceiling floated in the air. The long-legged, green bugs listened. The bamboo sounded like wings beating in the wind.

"Yes, I would like this, too," she said. "But I must tell my father." And she began taking off all the necklaces and bracelets.

"Keep them," he begged. "I want you to have them."

"No, no. I cannot," she said. "Not yet. Not until I am your wife."

But Chang the Good's hand folded over hers. "Keep the ring at least. Keep the ring in good faith until we can marry." And she agreed.

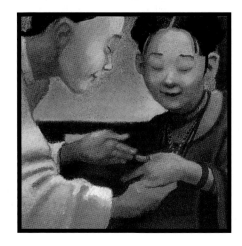

That night Kung Shi Fair went to her father, the father who had built her a moon pavilion and a boat when she asked, the very father who had built her a stone bridge when she wanted one, and the same father who had sent out servants to collect frogs for her. Knowing now that all those things were no longer what she truly wanted, she said to him, "I would marry now, Father."

And he answered, "Not yet, my daughter, not yet."

At that moment, a servant ran into the room.

"There is more news, Master, from down the river. The wild leopard is coming closer. It has killed more people. It leaves death everywhere."

"This is terrible," the merchant said. "Find out how close the leopard is."

"Yes, Master," the servant answered, and he backed out of the room.

Kung Shi Fair had barely heard the servant. "But, Father, you have always been so good to me. And this is what I want more than anything. If not now, then when?"

The merchant ran his hand over the top of his head and stared sadly out the window. "When the first call of the migrant geese is heard over the land, when the cicadas are still. And maybe you should stay away from your pavilion for a while."

"Oh, Father," she sighed, but he held up his hand and would hear no more.

Kung Shi Fair could not get married without her father's permission, but she did not stay away from her moon pavilion. Chang the Good was not discouraged by the news of her father's reluctance. One day when he was leaving, he told her, "Summer is nearly over, so we will wait for the migrating geese."

Laughing and turning his boat out into the gentle current, he promised to crush beneath his foot every cicada he could find until there was not a single one left. Kung Shi Fair stood on the shore and watched him sail away. Across the river, for the first time, she saw the village children waving to her, and feeling hopeful, she waved back.

Autumn came quickly that year, bringing sudden cool evenings and a fast churning river. Kung Shi Fair was having dinner with her father one night when she heard a distant honking. She leapt to her feet. "Father! Father! Come out on the terrace," and he, knowing, hearing the geese himself, reluctantly walked out beside her. They stood together, heads back, and watched the geese fly overhead.

"Now?" she whispered. "Now can I be married?"

"Not yet, my daughter, not yet."

She stared at him in disbelief. "Then when?"

"When I find a copper coin in my path," he said.

"Oh, Father, that is not fair. How will I know if you find a copper coin in your path? You will keep it from me!"

But at this her father held up his hands to silence her. "Enough!" he shouted, and he turned away.

With the sound of the honking geese still ringing in her ears, Kung Shi Fair ran from the room to hide her tears, past the servant who was coming to tell the merchant that the leopard was terribly close.

Chang the Good could not be discouraged. Sitting in Kung Shi Fair's moon pavilion, he thought of a plan. He did not stay that day for he had special work to do, and he told Kung Shi Fair to sit by her window at dawn.

The next morning, Kung Shi Fair watched the rain paint little jewels on her hands as she leaned on the window. Her father was preparing to go to a village meeting concerning the rampaging leopard. She saw the servants bring the carriage around to him, and just as her father was about to climb on, he looked down and saw coins strewn at his feet— hundreds of little copper coins. He looked up at his daughter in the window.

She saw no anger in his face, just sadness. She smiled kindly at him. "Now, Father? Can I now?"

He shook his head. "Not yet, my daughter, not yet."

Her smile turned to tears that mingled with the rain. "Then when, Father? Oh, then when?"

"When there's a rainbow over the stone bridge that leads to your moon pavilion," he told her, and he drove away.

Later the servants claimed to have heard Kung Shi Fair's sad crying that morning, even above winds that whistled over the river's surface. They told how Kung Shi Fair was brokenhearted, and that it was more than she could bear. They decided she had gone to find Chang the Good, to tell him his plan had failed.

The village women later whispered about how she went down to the bank of the tumbling Wen River, to her boat that had never been wet. She had watched many times as Chang the Good had pushed off the bank and sailed away, and now—hoping she could remember how, just from watching—she awkwardly pushed her boat of cassia, fig leaves, and orchid banners into the surging river.

Turning her young and determined face into the wind, she steered bravely through the river's foam and rapids. She rode the river's swells and currents. But this is the sad part of the story, and perhaps the worst part, because when she was halfway across the river, the wind ripped the fig leaf sails from their mast, and the orchids were torn and bruised, and the cassia bark hull snapped apart, tipping the merchant's beautiful daughter into the torrential river. For a few moments her silken robe could be seen floating near the surface, and then it was gone.

In the village, knowing there would be a storm, Chang the Good had not gone down to his boat that morning. Instead he had gone to the village meeting to hear the news about the rampaging leopard. Everyone was in great turmoil, frightened that the leopard would come right into their village and kill their families. Chang the

Good noticed that Kung Shi Fair's father was there, and he smiled to himself thinking of all the coins the merchant must have found at his feet that morning. But Chang the Good did not speak. In time, he was sure Kung Shi Fair would present him to her father, so he stayed at the back of the hall and listened. The villagers were clearly upset, wringing their hands and crying. Then the merchant spoke to them.

"While the storm is raging," he said, "we must go out, seek the leopard, and slay him before he comes to our village and kills again."

"Yes!" "Yes!" the villagers cried. "We will find the leopard before he finds us!" "Kill the leopard now!"

Chang the Good had thoughts only for Kung Shi Fair. He had no heart for a hunt. Without being seen, he stepped out into the rain, walked slowly to stand beneath a pear tree, and turned his eyes to the river. He thought to himself how once the rain stopped and the winds calmed, he would sail over and see her and ask her how things had gone with her father and the coins.

Meanwhile the swords were brought out and the bows and arrows, the spears and the clubs, and everyone received a weapon. The villagers poured out of the hall, out of every house and temple, and they took to the rain-slick road, in search of the leopard.

It was dark when the winds finally calmed and the river slowed its fury. Out of habit, the cormorant perched on the back of Chang the Good's boat, as he eased it into the river. Chang the Good gave it a final push and jumped in. Slowly and carefully, he made his way across, peering into the darkness of the pavilion to see if Kung Shi Fair waited for him. But there was no sign of her.

He pulled his boat ashore and called, "Kung Shi!" There was silence.

He ran up the shore and to the bridge, the cormorant flapping behind him. "Kung Shi!"

He ran to the pavilion and threw back the rain-soaked silks. "Kung Shi!"

Frightened, he turned toward her father's house that was dark and lifeless. His feet barely touched the ground. The cormorant shrieked and swooped after him. At the threshold of the house, he called again, and when there was no answer, he entered. He ran from room to room, calling her name and hearing the silence answer. He knew something terrible had happened. But he did not know what it was.

Slowly he left the house. The song of the small green frogs carried him to the stone bridge and he decided to sit there and wait for her. Surely she would come back to him soon. She would walk across this bridge and find him. He sat silently with the cormorant beside him, her black wings spread. The moon slipped out of the clouds and hung in the willow, polishing the water beneath his dangling feet.

Suddenly the cormorant flapped her wings and shrieked. She peered into the water. "Not now," Chang the Good told her. "Tomorrow we work."

But she did not listen to him. Before he could stop her, the cormorant dived into the water and disappeared into the shimmering darkness. Then in a spray of water she flew straight up and landed beside Chang the Good. She was not obliged to turn over her catch, but she dropped what she was carrying into her master's hand.

It was a small, jade thumb ring.

Chang the Good saw it and at that moment, he knew. He jumped up, and his eyes searched the shore for the cassia boat with the fig leaf sails and the orchid banners and he knew. He saw the whole story before him and threw back his head. He knew it was too late.

Just as the moon began to slip into sight, the weary villagers were returning home empty-handed. They were uneasy with the hunt, anxious to be back with their children and their oxen, their wives and their homes. There had been no leopard to kill, no prey for their hunt. They mumbled that perhaps it had all been a rumor.

As they came back toward the village, they heard a sound coming from across the water near the merchant's house. "The leopard!" they whispered, fingering their spears. "We must kill him!" At that, three of them jumped into a boat and sailed silently across the river to the place where the sound came from.

Now for many years after, the villagers tried to describe to each other what the sound was like. Some said it was a

lonely wailing. Others said it was like the sound of a trapped animal just before it dies. Most thought it sounded like the ragings of a rampaging leopard before it strikes. Later they all knew it was the sound of Chang the Good, crying his heart into the night.

Silently the boat slipped onto the river bank, and the three men crept up the shore. In the moonlight they saw their enemy. On the bridge, in the silver reflection of the river they saw a leopard with savage teeth and murderous claws. In one thrust they all shot arrows, threw spears, and sent clubs sailing through the wailing air. Their mark was made, and Chang the Good toppled into the river beneath the bridge.

If this was the end of the story, it would probably have been forgotten by now, it was so long ago. But because the merchant was so heartbroken, he cried his sorrows to whomever would listen to him, and the entire village soon knew he had kept his daughter away from the man she loved by demanding a rainbow over the stone bridge that led to her moon pavilion.

It was some time later, while the last leaves were still on the willow, turning yellow from cool evenings, that there was a cloudburst in the late afternoon. The merchant was at his scrolls, writing with black ink and an empty heart, when he heard the villagers cry out on the opposite shore of the river, and he went to the window.

His heart leapt at the sight, for just above the foot bridge that led to his daughter's pavilion, there appeared a most wondrous rainbow of every color, and while the villagers watched, and while the merchant watched, two swallows fluttered above the willow tree and kissed, their wings making the sound of wind in bamboo.

In order that this story never be forgotten, the merchant commissioned a plate be made to tell the story. The village artist, who had known Chang the Good and loved him like a brother, did a fine painting of the merchant's mansion, the village across the river, Chang the Good's boat, the moon pavilion, and the three hunters on the bridge. He did not paint a leopard, for after the storm no one ever heard of the leopard again, and many wondered if it had existed at all.

But over the willow tree he placed the two swallows in flight at the moment they kissed. Around them he tried to paint a border of what the rainbow had looked like, and around that border another border with the designs that had been on the simple jewelry that Chang the Good had offered to Kung Shi Fair.

When the plates were finished, the merchant gave them to everyone in the village and anyone who came through the village. He said he did it so that parents everywhere would always listen to their children, and would always, always heed what was in their children's hearts.

The Blue Willow plate was created in the eighteenth century in England, during a time when the English and other Western Europeans were much influenced and inspired by Chinese culture. The legends of what became one of the world's most beloved patterns followed the creation of the plate itself, exciting across the centuries the imagination of teller after teller.

Still, just as the plate has certain basic elements that always appear (the willow tree, the bridge, the tea house), so certain elements always appear in the story: the wealthy Chinese father who wishes his daughter to marry a man he has chosen, the daughter, usually Hong Shee or Koong Shee, who is in love with another younger man, and Chang, the younger man. The young lovers in the tale are thwarted and the suitor, or both the suitor and the daughter, die and the gods turn them into turtledoves. Now the two lovers can be together forever.

Pam Conrad came to the legend through a plate that had been in her own family. I believe it is fair to say, the plate enchanted her. And one day, when her own daughter was on the edge of adulthood and discovering young love, Pam wrote her own "legend." Yes, it contains the basic elements of the traditional story, but Pam's tale went beyond, touching with love and passion the deepest chord between parents and their children who must grow up, and away.

Because this story was so deeply personal to her, this legend of the Blue Willow held a special place in her heart.

—*Patricia Lee Gauch*, friend and editor

The publisher wishes to thank Dennis Grafflin in the Department of History at Bates College for his kind help in researching many details of Chinese history.

Text copyright © 1999 by Pam Conrad. Illustrations copyright © 1999 by S. Saelig Gallagher.
Philomel Books, Reg. U.S. Pat. & Tm. Off. Published simultaneously in Canada.

Printed in Hong Kong by South China Printing Co. (1988) Ltd.

Book design by Cecilia Yung and Gunta Alexander. The text is set in 12 point Cochin.

The artist would like to thank Alice Tang for the calligraphy.

The artwork was done in acrylic, pastel and mixed media on Arches rag paper.

Library of Congress Cataloging-in-Publication Data

Conrad, Pam. Blue Willow / Pam Conrad : illustrated by S. Saelig Gallagher. p. cm.
Summary: Kung Shi Fair's wealthy father gives her everything she asks of him; but when she requests permission to marry, he learns too late the value of listening.
[1. Fathers and daughters—Fiction. 2. Listening—Fiction.] I. Gallagher, Susan, ill.
II. Title PZ7.C76476B 1999 [Fic]—dc20 95-42867 CIP AC
ISBN 0-399-22904-3 (hc) 10 9 8 7 6 5 4 3 2 1

First Impression

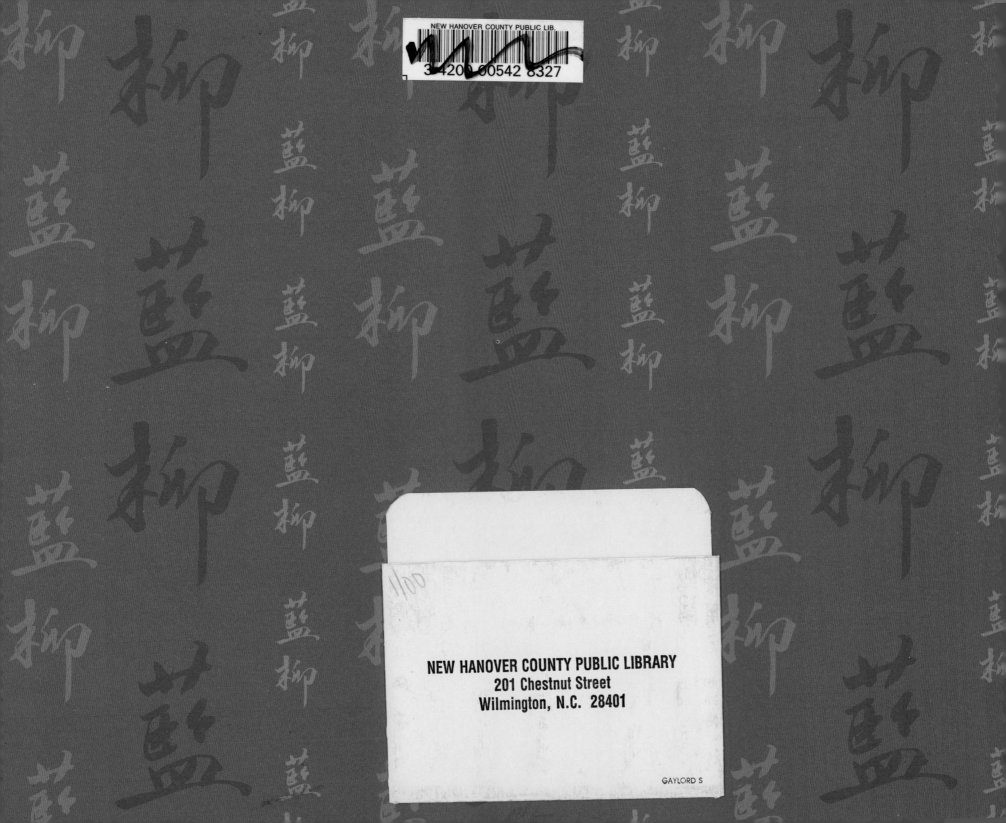